THE PRESENCE

"A suspenseful thriller . . . provocative . . . nicely done, indeed."

—*Kirkus Reviews*

"Enough smoothly crafted suspense to keep readers turning pages long after dark."

—*The Seattle Times*

BLACK LIGHTNING

"Electrifyingly scary."

—San Jose *Mercury News*

"One of Saul's best."

—*Publishers Weekly*

THE HOMING

"If you are a Stephen King/Dean Koontz fan, *The Homing* is a book you will only open once. You will not put it down until its last page has been absorbed. John Saul takes the psychological suspense novel to a new height."

—*The Dayton Voice*

GUARDIAN

"Chills and thrills . . . a great hair-raiser."

—*San Diego Union-Tribune*

BY JOHN SAUL

SUFFER THE CHILDREN
PUNISH THE SINNERS
CRY FOR THE STRANGERS
COMES THE BLIND FURY
WHEN THE WIND BLOWS
THE GOD PROJECT
NATHANIEL
BRAINCHILD
HELLFIRE
THE UNWANTED
THE UNLOVED
CREATURE
SECOND CHILD
SLEEPWALK
DARKNESS
SHADOWS
GUARDIAN
THE HOMING
BLACK LIGHTNING

THE BLACKSTONE CHRONICLES
PART ONE: *An Eye for an Eye: The Doll*
PART TWO: *Twist of Fate: The Locket*
PART THREE: *Ashes to Ashes: The Dragon's Flame*
PART FOUR: *In the Shadow of Evil: The Handkerchief*
PART FIVE: *Day of Reckoning: The Stereoscope*
PART SIX: *Asylum*

THE PRESENCE
THE RIGHT HAND OF EVIL
NIGHTSHADE
THE MANHATTAN HUNT CLUB
MIDNIGHT VOICES
BLACK CREEK CROSSING
PERFECT NIGHTMARE